She Wanted Storms

a collection of poetry and short stories

by Annette Marie Smith

First Printing: 2016

ISBN: 978-0692726815

Lucky Horseshoe Publishing
2285 University Ave. W.
Saint Paul, MN 55114

www.annettemariesmith.com

*It's raining so hard that
all the windows shudder
with delight.*
— AMS

Contents

Acknowledgements

Special thanks to the following publications where these pieces first appeared:
Thrush Poetry Journal ~ "Lake Calhoun"
Iodine Poetry Journal ~ "Rain and Darkness Fall"
Full of Crow Magazine ~ "earlier, then, now"
Empowerment4Women Magazine ~ "spirits on the wind and with a noise"
DoveTales Literary Journal ~ "Come Spring"
Empowerment4Women Magazine ~ "you think"
Empowerment4Women Magazine ~ "the big melt"
DoveTales Literary Journal ~ "Forgiveness Finds Me"
Fantasy and Fairytales Magazine ~ "Constant Melusine"

She Wanted Storms

*Poems to Be Read
to the Music of the Rain*

Annette Marie Smith

Sunday Morning Rain Storm

My bed, an island of Eden
a silk tent raised
a downy castle.
The storm of the world shaking
all around us
the sky arching like a rusted metal sheet
while the torrential rain rumbles
your name
trembling its syllables into my marrow.
Your arms are a portculis of protection.
Your stones were each floated into place by Merlin himself.
I take it as a compliment when you call me Nimue
say I ride the storm like it is my own broom
accuse me of being your undoing.
But I have come
not to imprison you
in tree, in cave, in arrested state,
my love, I have come
to set you free.

She Wanted Storms

Wild horses

with lightning hooves
thunder by my window
stampede on the roof
and shake
their dark clouds of mane –
Mustang rain.

Glass Slippers

"The rain," I heard her say
"fits my feet perfectly
better than any glass slipper
you could ever dream."

She Wanted Storms

Silver minnows swim

down the stream of my window pane
gleam against the dark mountains of storm
overhead
shiver like magic flowing by me.

Annette Marie Smith

No Need for a Lee

Snowflakes flutter their diamond prismed wings,
stir a hurricane of chills
up and down my spine.
From halfway across the world
you call me with soft rain in your voice.
Thoughts of you floteren, then flood me,
a tropical stormfront moving in.

Miniature leaves

looking like a thousand of the tiniest birds in the world
made of sunshine and photosynthesis
and flower's voices on the breeze,
they flew by followed by a shower of petals.
I could hardly stand to walk on the storm left in my path.

Untitled

The dark sky is filled with fireflies.
My heart is barefoot beneath the moon.

She Wanted Storms

dream poem

the silk of this night
is like sheets tangled around my feet
you pull those sheets up and over us
with your teeth.
the night has become a private tent
for us to wander with hands and tongue beneath
the arch of sky dark with desire
what land!
what lakes!
what aurora borealis we!
what way we lose ourselves upon
beneath the wind tossed trees!

Annette Marie Smith

Lake Calhoun
(after Ezra Pound's "In a Station of the Metro", Paris 1913)

The reflection of these faces by the lake;
Glints that gleam in a wave's wake.

Everglade Drifting

After the rain,
sugarcane runs long fingers
through the sky's curly clouds.
Gators spank the river bank
with disciplinary tails.
Mosquitoes drape the shoreline
like Spanish Moss hanging on the trees.
The sky is a bleached denim blue
so soft
I decide to wear just that –
like a favorite old frayed shirt –
as I drift in my canoe.

Caer Ibormeith

Often and often has my wild nature taken me over
like some witch-cast spell
taking me over and giving me over
to fiáin primitive things.
Swan Maiden they call me
and yes I rue the impetuousness
but never the free-flung wings.

Shells are the bones of the sea

and that is why you can hear chanting
like ghostly whispers from the other side
undulating against your ear
when you hold a shell up to it.
And salt is the sea's kiss.
Once you've tasted it
you can't imagine even the simplest joys of life without it.
The moonlight on the sea is heart's own memory
peeking through ragged clouds and gracing
even Charybdis swells with grace.
You are a metaphor made up of longing
strong enough to pull a tide and raise the dead,
to shake seashell bones and tumble pearls from their tight
beds
and yet quietly lap
at the edges of my dreams leaving me
to wake with the lessons of salt and mystery
upon my lips.

Annette Marie Smith

Words

Words have paper hands.
They light their hands on fire
to illuminate the meaning they are chanting
with their tongues made up of silver bells
while their feet do the Harlem shuffle.
With apologies to Emily, words, really,
are the things with feathers that sing and sing and sing.
Words congregate thickly, like a murder of crows,
on the branch of a poet's brow.
Your branches are thick and wild,
heavy with the howls of wolves.
Your forest is inked darkly,
a tattoo on the muscled forearm skyline
of this cardboard and concrete nature preserve.

All The Flames

The night comes in the same way that Odin travels the
roads and paths between the worlds:
portended from afar,
his heavy walking stick booming
as it hits the cobblestones of stars,
and yet a surprise in sudden arrival.
Street lamps flicker on of their own accord
as my hand makes the sign of peace
that the stroke of a light switch can be.
All the flames — sulfur, incandescent,
sodium vapor,and more — all the flames dance in welcome.

There is a fire in the ice,

in the blue water beneath the thin glass.
Its flame is gelid and sings
of sharp sleep, a lucid dream.

She Wanted Storms

He is an ark,

they said,
and he will carry you
over those troubled waters.
He is safe and heaven sent.
But she leapt from his wooden arms
and over the side and into the churning sea
and reveled
in what had been called folly
but felt like every kind of free.
The long shadow of his prow
followed her, an accusatory finger.
And he had two of every kind of net
and two by two of every kind of sharp edged thing
with which to hunt beneath the moon.

We Are All, All of Us Souls, Boats

We find ports that call to us. We anchor. We dock.
But the sea is always there and the sea is always calling.
It is inevitable that we will unfurl our sails, like wings, and
take to the tides again.
Come Scylla and Charybdis, come Kraken,
come Selkie and Siren, and all unplumbed depths.
Even the Death Sea is not the last sea. — *Eller Oarsson of
Landsend from the Night Fairytale Series*

She Wanted Storms

Voie Périlleuse

Even the stars blurred the night I left you.
My cape, red as intent,
propelled me down a path that seemed unreal,
with trees that looked as if they were etched
by an artist's hand.
But they came to life, the trees,
breathed and rustled and burgeoned
into a forest behind me
as I made my way beneath the pregnant moon.
They sighed gustlets of wind as they stirred.
Fluttering handkerchiefs to catch each falling sorrow,
or scrubbing pads to scour
every image of you from the very heart of me?
I still cannot be sure.

Annette Marie Smith

The Stuff of Dreams and Beams

The new moon has its own night terrors:
Its milky toes juxtaposed with the pinching hinges
of tree branch traps,
the precision balance
required to navigate
heaven, horizon, and poet's eye;
an inexhaustible quiver
of silver arrows paired
with the wolves of clouds hungry, howling,
for just such stuff.

Toadstone and Iron

Leaves shake like so many chatelaines
while the wind speaks to me in the language of keys
turns the tumbler that holds the spirit lock in place
conjures dancers made of rust and gold
sets them to dance and grace unfolds.
Whither widdershins so bold?

Annette Marie Smith

Selkie Shift

I wore a dress made of paper
It rustled when I walked. You were the wind
pulling at it, creeping with fingers of cold
trying to get under my skin.
I came dressed in mud, painted obscure as night.
You were the chain that pulled on the light.
I wore birdsong
and dawn was a crown in my hair.
You came with a lawnmower and blade-spread
feathers everywhere.
I took off my skin and wore spirit to escape you
but you stole my skin like I was a selkie
making me feel I could never go home
would always be prisoned with you –
why I left when I could.

Wolves

May your wolves walk on the path with you
where you can see them.
May they swirl with mane of mist with leaves
caught twined therein.
May you hear that their wildness calls
to you
that their teeth portend tools
as well as menace
that their howls are not just hunting jargon
but sonnets to the moon.

Spring Rain

It rained last night and the drops
are still scattered on my window panes.
The rain kisses all things mundane and beautiful,
from roses to blacktop.
Maybe that is one of the reasons
we want to tip our faces into the rain,
to be a part of the benediction.

The Clouds Are Speckled Koi

Raindrops kiss the window's face,
plink into the welcoming arms
of the waters of the lake,
shiver along branches
and shimmer as they fall
like tiny shooting stars
inside a waterfall.

In the Air Tonight

Street dreams and petrichor –
that smell you get after rain –
are in the air tonight.
Diesel rainbows flutter in puddles
looking for all the world like liquid butterflies
while the rain, a thousand tiny hummingbirds,
beats against each flower pane.
I open my window and let them fly in.

tipping the delivery guy
(another rain poem)

the sky fumbles in her purse
looking for change
to tip the moon with
(you can't get better delivery
than he has provided this month)
and spills all her shiny silver coins
into the street below

Annette Marie Smith

Preach It!

Raindrops hurrying along
all going to the big underground church
with the best echoes
for the choir singing "stormy waters"
and the stained glass windows of their prisms
wink and flash for the diluvial congregation
that holy-roller thunders through the pipes
of a sewer system that is an organ
that can hold those service notes in-definitely
and amplify the sermon's message that
something as gentle as a raindrop
when joined with its brethren and its sistren
can be as mighty as the sea.

Call it a washout summer flooding
of wet epiphany.

She Wanted Storms

Where it belongs,

right up there with the birds and with the rain
before it even falls.
It's hard to get your head out of the clouds
if that's where it intrinsically belongs.

Annette Marie Smith

Headlights Float Like Candles

Headlights float like candles
On a dark river
While tires break the mirrored surface of the road
Over and over again
Sending the candled reflections,
Shivery slivers that are made up
Of moments between raindrops,
Rushing for the sea.

She Wanted Storms

I don't know if anyone ever told you,

but the cars actually like it when it rains.
They like splashing through the puddles
and using their wipers and defrosters
with their radios turned down low.
They like the way the water just slides
right off them as they ski on hydroplanes
how refracted light makes blurry paintings of them
everywhere they go. Their pride in showing off
to perfection their brakes and inside environment control
is something to behold. Even slow cars, even rusty,
one-eyed cars that are old, can't help but put their shine on
when the rain starts to unfold.

Annette Marie Smith

Rain and Darkness Fall

The rain rides the night's shoulders
like Puck riding the back of a great owl
that sweeps the sky with the absence of light,
turning off the moon and covering up the eyes
of all the stars. The shadow of night's dark wings falls
while Puck shoots all the arrows he has
and the feathered raindrops spin
like fishermen's lures
in the eddying stream flowing down my window.
The pages of the book that I am writing
are paper curtains that I draw against the dimness
outside the lamp-lit room that is my mind.
But paper loves water, will drink it thirstily, and I
find myself making curtains into boats
to launch on a rainy sea.

She Wanted Storms

the sky

scatters sunshine by the handful today
like a king of old tossing coins
to the populace at large
and those coins float
like liquid candles
on the puddles from the storm
plash-meres that are mirrors
filled with peonies
and I want to look in every one
hold my face so that those
peonies turn to roses
reflecting on my throat remembrances
of darkness swirled with gold

earlier, then, now

earlier

clouds thick with blueberry shadows
curled around ribbons of cream

then

the rain repetitively rattled the window
like someone with OCD

now

petals layer the walkway
a special event red carpet — for nobody but the wind

She Wanted Storms

Rain Rave

Bead curtains (strung raindrops)
looking like Christmas lights in their blurry-hurry
hang against my windows, turn and sway with the wind
letting me peek over the looming shoulder
of the storm
(the storm is a bouncer just looking for trouble).

It's a dark club outside tonight
with techno rhythm rain
and glow stick patterns
made by car taillights.
'Tornado' stands at the club entrance –
he'll stamp your hand
and keep it
as he thunder-mumbles that the drinks
are on the house.

The street's a dance floor.
I stand back, press my fingertips
against the window glass
touching mini tocsins that pulse
each beat of rain sounding alarums
through the night.
I leave the dancing to the swinging traffic lights
and other weed-whipped things that shake in unison
while the show-off shadows dance alone.

Annette Marie Smith

spirits on the wind and with a noise –

like knuckle bones rattling in a tin cup
like shivers written with silver music –
comes the rain against the pane

while each windy wail huffs like hot breath
leaving condensation on blurred windows
(the eyes of the house are clogged with tears)

the clouds, dark hood, hang over the building's head
and chill is a skeleton key
that can open any door
(hinges creak and loose boards tremble in this downpour)

but the heart of the home glow –
every light in the place turned on –
and matches strike a ready pose

in case candle cannon is called for
to blast away darkness when electricity fails
in such a tempest onslaught of bad-dream-storm

poem for a rainy night

tonight
the wind tells secrets to the trees
teaches all the thirsty leaves
tossing black silver and green

that tempest can carry
canting truths, toss branches high
in rush crushed rue
then leave them still, serene
in the middle of the eye
of the storm

where does grace come from?
where does bending blend
to strength and the ability to weather
thunderous calamity?

tonight
a cat with fur on end
will come in from the wind
knowing in its catty ways
that the storm is not for him

and better sieged with lapping tongue
to saucer dipped
than drops of rain on skin
of nose or whiskers fierce

will sit on sill and watch
the arboreal trembling
now with not one hair awry

Annette Marie Smith

rainy october monday

the rustle of paper
that is really leaves
shuffling, shuffling
above my head
crumpled at my feet

a dripping ink sky
black blue and gray
the font is rain
and writes/splashes
on everything

the weather as poet
rainy october monday

She Wanted Storms

makeup artist

rain shimmers highlights on branches
glosses the lips of the leaves
applies intense blue shadow to the lake shore lid
precipita-cosmetically
gives the day a makeover so intense
it looks like a photo-shopped picture
on the cover of a magazine

Annette Marie Smith

Sweep Me Away

Snowflakes dance outside my window
kiss the cold glass pane
like moths drawn to a flame
they melt in a fatal embrace.

The steam from my breath
on my frosty windowpane
makes my mind's eye see
the heat rise off your skin
like morning mist off the sea

and you are like a merman
in the depths you can reach
the things you can teach.
I just want to be caught
in your nets, in your arms, in your charms.

Sweep me away
to crystal caves
beneath the waves
and regale me with stories
written in the smallest of pearls
on the rarest abalone
kept in chests sunk long years ago.

Just pull me down with you
we'll breath as one, we two.
I wont want for gills
because I'll be with you.

She Wanted Storms

Weather Report: Foggy, Rainy, Dark

It's true that fog wrapped the buildings in its embrace
sweated the windows and lapped the necks
of every person in the city who was out and about today.

I'm sorry about that – but you made me hot.
And the darkness of the day? I closed my eyes
and the whole city closed its eyes with me.
But the rain was not my fault.

Keep Talking

Awash in the whitecaps
of your words
my resistance is a fleet
of paper boats
that sinks
gently unfolding like a sigh
or a whisper told under water.
My boats drift to the bottomless depths
lost in a sea of persuasion.

Untitled

Your are the wind.
You have me spinning widdershins.
My thoughts are leaves arush and atumble
in the current of you.

For the Looking Through

I like your clean eyes.
They are windows that are for the looking through.
The vista is wild and beautiful
just like you.

She Wanted Storms

The sky is green like your eyes and full of storms,
(for my Da)

lightning and thunder and rain.
Thoughts of you cascade
in lime colored diamonds
rattling my windowpanes.
Wild calls with her siren song
her voice wind-raspy as she moans out my name.
She rides bareback and her hands are laced
in her horse's feral mane.
What I think of
on a tempestuous night like this
is of you and your robin-breast hair
how I'd love to run out and ride the storm with you
a father and daughter pair.

Annette Marie Smith

Fire Speaks in Many Tongues

Fire speaks in many tongues
all of them universal.
Water uses interpretive dance.

"You make my mind dance." He said
Let our minds dance together, I thought,
and our bodies too.

Let the fire of passion caress
and let the sweat beads drop
sizzling beside your hands on me
and mine on you
with flames that dervish whirl
whisk me away in blue-white heat
and set my mind to sea
with waves that rock our mutual boats
mu-si-cal-ly.

She Wanted Storms

Aillte Bána

The sound of rain swept into my consciousness
this morning
bringing with it thoughts of you to waken me
from walking along the steep white cliffs of sleep.
There was not one blade of green to be seen
as far as the eye could see
on the endless cliffs of dream
but I saw the full St. Patrick's day moon
far out on the horizon
poised between the heavens and the sea
and I felt the rustle of emerald grass
whole hillsides shivered
and sparkled like glass
in the island of my heart
as the rain fell this morning
and I woke to thoughts of you and me.

Annette Marie Smith

Stone Cold: A Mermaid's Lament

You, stone statue chisel perfect
and impervious that you are,
what happened?
How did you end up here
under the waves
of aquamarine music that scrolls
above and around you –
where the ripples tinkle like laughter
and the riptides have their way?

If ever a siren sang
she sang to you.
If ever someone couldn't resist
that someone would have to be you.
I see the seaweed making tracks
and everywhere its fingers trace
along your marble torso
the seaweed fingers point to cracks
highlighting them and more so
showing me things by the sea's eerie light
within your sculpted shadow
showing me things, truth be told
I do not want to know.
Tooth of coral
and wing of ray
let my eyes not see.
Tooth of coral
and wing of ray
let my eyes not see.

Was it my song took you under
that I sang in the midst of the salty storm?
I wouldn't have sung at all

48

She Wanted Storms

if I knew it would weave such wrong.
La! Lachrymose boats,
the salt of tears a needful thing
in stiffening their sails,
skim the dark horizon –
an albatrossic swale.

All fulsome floating breasts
contrived of wood or flesh
swell and heave –
surging wreckaged loss.
The other mermaids know,
wringing handfuls to buckets
out of hair and eyes,
just how much it takes
to make a painted prow-smile cry.
Before you were cold and stiff
under here with me
did you drink in the sunshine's nectar
through your every single pore?
Tooth of coral
and wing of ray
let my eyes not see.
Tooth of coral
and wing of ray
let my eyes not see.

The greedy seagulls have given up
glib glide and swallow,
their breezy acrobatic wallow,
and sit immobile on the shore.
Without legs I can't do more
than linger near the outer bay
in the tide-pool's ebb and sway
counting out the rhythmic beat

49

of every wave's foray

thinking of men who once walked about
whereas now they simply lie
some further along to statues of bones
down in the darkness with Davy Jones.
The very next storm – this I swear –
I'll sing not one word and thus I'll spare
more statues littering my playground.
This I vow, I'll make not a sound
and let me be by Neptune bound.
Tooth of coral
and wing of ray
let my eyes not see.
Tooth of coral
and wing of ray
let my eyes not see.

Driftwood Tells Its Story
(Blanchir)

Buoyed by salt and hollowed out by time,
I am driftwood
and I have made my way to shore.
Would you know yet more?
The bones of me sing upon the wind.
I have become a flute, a type of carved out reed
an intimate piece of musical instrument art –
hand-crafted by the sea.
My stag horns and fluers-de-lis rear wildly towards the sky
while my pale feet dip among the wavelet's small sighs.
My secret is imbued in every grain of me.
My great beauty comes from having drowned
but come back from the deeps.
I have weathered storms
and I have left a world of green behind.
Leaves and roots mean nothing now
to the likes of me
but the color I seemingly left behind
is hidden steeped in me
and when I burn upon a fire
new colors are set free.
Grass green and sky blue
and dancing yellow citrine
bloom like flowers as they flame
from my wan and twisted branches
by the roaring sea.

Annette Marie Smith

Red Shoes, Dolls, and Merrow Trees

Some day my impulsivity, my spontaneity, will be the
storybook red shoes that dance my feet right off of me.

I am not the handless maiden, but I might as well just be,
for all the grasp I have wearing gloves of naivety.

In the courtyard of my thoughts, a tree lined twisting maze,
there is an Ariadne thread. I find it in your gaze.

Sometimes given context dolls are scary things; after all,
they started out as idols and the kind of gods that let you
carry them are likely full of pins.

I am more inclined to seek the benediction of your smile
than look for hope in talismans or relics full of guile.

In a forest full of merrow trees there is the underwater
sheen of moon kissed waves that lave the very heart of
dream.

Romantic Wrecks and Sea Dreams

The sky is made of sea dreams this evening
doubloons wink as early stars
pearl and half-shell clouds drift
across the deep sky
and the wavering light ripples like liquid
like waves lapping gently
in a current from the tops of the pearls
to the tips of the trees
some bare, some flowering
and all of them looking like branches of coral
in a romantic underwater wreck

Annette Marie Smith

broken things
(for Jensen)

you love the burnt things
the broken wings
the missing pieces
the shattered hearts wrapped up
with bandages and twine

you just know that somewhere
in the soot, in the ashes
in the detritus and wreck
are hidden things, overlooked
treasures all the brighter
for having been through trial and fire

I see you collecting lost souls
like butterflies in jars
without lids
so they can fly out anytime they want
your heart is a magnifying glass
that makes everyone else's look all the bigger
your eyes illuminate their dark corners
turning spider webs to fairy-flax

your hands carry smoke and splinters
transmuted to bars of gold and perfumed incense

little black bird

little black bird
singing through the night
you are up late just like me
beneath the blankets of starlight

I am writing with pen and paper
you are scribbling on the air
we both compose while others sleep
we are an inky pair

Annette Marie Smith

Delicate Instrument

Imagine my ardor for you
as a delicate instrument
a delicate instrument of desire
finely wrought
intricately fashioned
like some old fashioned pocket watch
with fabulous properties
and sweeping hands
that brush the finely carved face
that measures not minutes or hours
but sighs and exhalations of delight.

Well you took that beautiful artifact
and crushed it beneath your heel
and the glass splinters alone
sparkle achingly enough
to break the hands of time
but there is no putting it back together.

So now I'm feeling that my desire for you
was embarrassingly old-fashioned anyway
outdated in its romantic style.

Who needs it after all?
Give me a digital throwaway.

Bare Branches

I remember your tears falling
like leaves really
that left muddy tracks
down your cracked cheeks.

Those brittle eyes
that could shed such tears
so sere
and looking toward winter.

What could I do?
What could I do?
I pressed a kiss to my fingers
and then to your cheek
where it burrowed
a frightened thing

became a seed
with the promise of spring
if you could only water it
with something besides
your desiccated sorrow.

Annette Marie Smith

Unpredictable

The rain was falling like soft tears
but has hardened now into snow –
this can often happen with the heart
as well as with the weather.

Untitled

Sowing the whirlwind
and reaping the killing frost.
Sometimes though, the hurricaned wreckage
is worth the love we lost.

Annette Marie Smith

The Rain Sang Me To Sleep

The rain sang me to sleep last night
and washed away every thought of you.
Newly baptized by my own personal deluge
I woke this morning and the rain outside had stopped
but the rain inside is still beating
against the windows of my heart.
Meanwhile, the sidewalks of my mind glisten
all my lawns are wet
and my forests, draped in mist
beckon and reflect
the newly risen sun.

She Wanted Storms

Angels in the architecture

and ghosts in the machine,
swirling snow shows the dancing spirit
of the cold ice queen.
Polish my eyes with antimony.
Polish my eyes like stones.
Make me see the invisible
that lives beside my own.
Let the angels weep.
Let the ghosts gnash teeth.
Let the windows melt
into pools of midnight water
as the mad snow dances
to the ice queen's tune.

lullaby

and the ocean is rocking, rocking
her baby to sleep
while the stars in the sky
promise to keep
the heavens held like a canopy
to soar overhead
to ripple with all the breezes of dream
and never fall down, and never fall down
rest and drift asleep

High Winds Shake the Branches of My Tree of Dreams

My dreams flutter like leaves in the wind of night
flutter on a tree of dreams with whispering branches
that murmur in the storm.

The tree top touches the heavens.
Its roots snake down and down
while the lightning-forked sky shows
a slow wheeling shadow of wings
that brush against my senses.

My thoughts dance along the tree's branches
birds just waiting for their turn
to launch aloft and free fall
with a parachute of sleep strapped to their backs
they don't even need their pinions.

Annette Marie Smith

When the Wind Tries to Whisper Your Name

When the wind tries to whisper your name
I have already patterned myself on Odysseus
clever and wily.
I have plugged my ears with cotton
from the fields of apathy.
I have wrapped my head in wool from sheep
who view the world indifferently.
Those fields, those flocks, were yours.

I have given my eyes to the three grey sisters
just in case the moon tries to remind me of you.
Now they have no need to share one eye
amongst themselves.
They have one clouded marble
and two tear-washed blue.
My eyes saw only you.

I stitched an oilskin on top of my fair flesh
so the rain couldn't kiss me and remind me of you best
like the sound of quiet thunder muffled to disguise itself
as train wheels turning on the track of my spirit
and the long slow lonely whistle
that was your mating call.
My skin was tattooed with your touch.

Autumn Bridge

The autumn forest
wet with rain
is a lucid dream
where all the colors
shine like glass
that has been polished
in the wind.

Every leaf is a door
that shakes and shudders
trembling to be opened
and behind which stand
all the trees of time
immemorial.

Fire and rain blend,
become a gateway
or a bridge
spanning from one season
to the next —
inviting one to cross.

Annette Marie Smith

At the End of the Rainbow

The rain streams in jewels down the window
clinks its coins on the street.

I turn away from its showy display of wealth
to trace the path of space between us.
My eyes mark the rainbow curve
that arcs from me and ends at you.

Are you the pot of gold at the rainbow's end?
I'm Irish enough to reach for you.

She Wanted Storms

**While the Rain Came Down and Your Baggage
Rode Your Back**
(for Teddy)

The house was dark and empty
lit only by the flashings of the storm
and I knew that you were getting lost
'cause I am your protector
even now you're gone.
I wept for your figure disappearing in the storm
while the rain came down
and your bags rode piggy-back.

Parents and defenders didn't hear my call
as I ran through muddy mazes
to come between your fall
and you – determined to be gone.
Your footprints left their say
in a hurried message on the lawn
while the rain came down
and your bags rode piggy-back.

They rode your shoulders like a child
and I knew that you'd be gone
my sorrow at your going
was that you were not yet ready
for the darkness and the storm.

My sorrow was for you
and for the appearance of a train
while the rain came down
and your bags rode piggy-back.

It could have been the lead car
in a funeral procession

67

for all the joy it lit the night
despite circus curlicue moldings
and gold glitter painted bars
and you were in it like an animal
settling in its straw
and I wept though I understood
the lure of its draw
while the rain came down
and your bags rode piggy-back.

They rode your shoulders like a child
and I knew that you'd be gone
my sorrow at your going
was that you were not yet ready
for the darkness and the storm.

The promise of adventure
and the hint of being free
were almost just enough to also get to me
but I saw that there were bars
in front of the stars that were in your eyes
and I couldn't rattle through the night
in a train-car strewn with lies
while the rain came down
and your bags rode piggy-back.

They rode your shoulders like a child
and I knew that you'd be gone
my sorrow at your going
was that you were not yet ready
for the darkness and the storm.

I woke like Seger to the sound of thunder
and a cry upon my lips
your image still before me

She Wanted Storms

my heartbeat racing glyphs
with the rain in abeyance
and your bags around my hips.

They sway when I walk
hold me back apace
but I will never give up
on the winning of this race.
I will never give up
on the winning of this race.

Annette Marie Smith

Come Spring

The air is filled with tiny white umbrellas
spinning as they fall
and interspersed between them
are raindrops cold and shaped like tears.
They coat the tips of trees in chrysalides
beneath the falling snow.
Such glass cocoons will bud with leaves
which unfurl their wings like butterflies
to flutter in the breeze,
come spring.

Persephone Sleeping

Persephone sleeps.
It is that time of year when she is as much in limbo
as the frozen trees and lakes and silenced katydids.
She has dropped her scepter mid-flourish and swooned
to cushions made ready for her annual foray
into the long corridor that is a dream
that connects winter to the spring.

Her pomegranate lipstick
(a personal choice to flaunt and celebrate her scars)
curves along her lips in a soft smile
(ah pomegranate,
whose tiny seeds were sown like dragon's teeth
with, not warriors, but the whirlwind for her to reap).
Her lids are curtains drawn to shield the dream
of spring that all the flowers dream concomitantly too.

Her heavy lashes, an equal mix of wool and silk,
are tie-down sashes
that hold her eyelids to her cheeks.
She is left to use her pale hands
to trail along the narrow walls
which are bas-reliefed with roots and painted drear.
She walks up the long corridor, a greater Eurydice
but blind, gaining substance as she goes,
ghosting from one realm to this other.

Her yearly reemergence is,
and perhaps I am the first to tell you this,
a long sleepwalk out of hell, a lucid dream as well
one in which she knows she will awaken
on a bed of flowers beneath open skies
that draw her gaze to trace infinity.

71

She knows she has not left her other self behind.
She cannot. She carries the seeds
of death sewn cunningly in her hair.
Braided with maypole ribbons
and set to take flight into the air –
on the first zephyr breeze that comes along.
But those seeds also have within them
every brief splash and splurge of color
every petal yet unfurled.
Such is the weight of life and death
she carries in her curls
as she lies sleeping, chthonic/kore Persephone.

you think

you think
because i don't talk
about confetti petals
parade of flowers
zephyr wind zing
that i don't see or feel them
but i do
and carry my gaze
to stems and leaves
press my ear to roots
the quiet causation
behind the loud bloom
which is a pebble
in my mouth
an impediment to speech
something to suck on
such is my silence towards you

Annette Marie Smith

the big melt

birds startle behind your eyes
your mouth holds a flood
that wants to wash out
foam over the cliffs
of what is between us

and the rush of water
has things in it
some ice still from the winter
some dead trees and detritus

my words are snares for your birds
my smile holds bridges
small ones, wooden ones
not anything
architecturally stunning

but my small wooden bridges
will make a way across
and my snares have taken your birds
so go ahead – say it

She Wanted Storms

Reel

Let the cold mists swirl.
Let the shamrocks riffle in the breeze
on the hard white cliffs that tower
above the green seaweed.

Call the dark puca
with the whistling of a one-eyed stone.
Trace the burly hillside's shoulders
to reach the tor top throne.

There I'll point my face seaward
with my back against the wall
the happiest of fairytale princesses
to ever attend a ball.

The gorgeous waves beneath me
dance in seabed's ballroom
and the rolling hills beckon me
with their sumptuous costume

to kick my heels up in the grass
although my slippers be of glass
and sure as I am you know I will
kick them off and race down that hill!

Annette Marie Smith

summer sky

morning

the clouds are deckle edged paper
letting the light shine through in layers
tinted by the watercolors of the rains they're painted with

afternoon

white clouds billow in the breeze
I'm making a tent
under the summer sheets
hanging on the clothesline sky
I'll come out when I am ready
(when the day calls me in for dinner)
and you will see me by and by

early evening

a long line of white birds
gets lost against the equally white clouds
becoming hint and vague suggestion
of flight in the sky where such things –
floating, flying – are so ordinary as to fade into invisibility
right before your eyes
if you allow yourself to have a blind eye to the
commonplace

I look beneath the surface line
between nothingness and splendor
unwrapping wonder as I go

Summer Has Come

Flowers are twining her hair
like roses climbing a trellis.
Petals tumble
fat and slow like honey.
The wind shakes them
like a pale tremble of wheat

and Summer lets
her Rapunzel tresses
waterfall down the tower
in a golden sheet
of rippling sunlight.

Don't you want to grab a handful?

Annette Marie Smith

The Trees of Summer Knocked on My Heart

The trees of summer knocked on my heart.
It woodenly ignored them.
Blue skies came by in person.
My heart focused on its cerulean locks
of steel and would not be unbarred.
Rain rang the bell repeatedly impatient as a storm.
The door of my heart turned into glass
and let the rain slide down its face.
When you arrived
my heart made of itself
a door of hanging prayer beads.
They lifted of themselves
like hair upon a startled nape
and remain
suspended in the air.

She Wanted Storms

hungover sky

the clouds, puffy and multilayered,
are bags under the sky's eyes today
he stayed up too late – stars in his eyes
and a big moon grin on his face
intoxicated by the night

copper discs of light

bounce across the rumpled sheets of lake water
they are tricks of the visible spectrum that walk and skip
on the surface of the water like happy little jesuses
or gerridae made of light

Wind on the Grass

The grass trembles tympanicly
stretched across the ear of the earth
and shakes like a thunder sheet –
the kind used to make sound effects
for old-timey radio shows.
And the grass bows its many heads
then raises them and sings
as the wind whispers accompaniment
and promises seedlings wings.

Annette Marie Smith

dandy lions

with white windblown manes
roam urban and residential
serengetis
shake their heads and pounce
only
to float away on the breeze

two faced wind
(for the first day of fall)

all the skirts and dresses
flutter, flip and flap in the wind
like colorful birds
like bunches of butterflies
like leaves skirling
or clouds curling
clouds of silk, rayon, polyester and cotton
billow near the ground
pillow out from slender waists
or gallop like horses
around legs
are streams of fabric
running across knees, babbling over thighs
laughing and teasing of carefree days

but it is autumn now
and those who know can see
that the skirts also sway like bells
tolling november
hair rises on the wind
in warning
faces pinch and eyes shut
like the closing of a book
and the posture of those out on the street
on this blustery day
sends signs as clear as any found in almanac
they are bent forward and struggling
against the hard wind blocking their way
as geese make patterns like tea leaves
on the empty bowl of the sky

Annette Marie Smith

The Leaves, What Leaves There Are

The leaves look like gray mice
nibbling at the cold
and that might seem like an awful thought –
trees swinging with colorless mice
their paper sharp teeth all a-nibble –
but I find comfort in knowing
that they will rattle away
following the wind like it is a pied piper
and taking their ice whiskers with them.

She Wanted Storms

Susurrus

When I think of you I don't think of leaves spinning
like ballerinas in the air
on their way down to the ground
having let go of whip thin branch
and wearing brilliant colors,
so beautiful a compensation,
for what they must portend.
I am not ready to see you in gold and red
(it is not your season yet)
when green is so fresh
and is the way I always picture you —
new and bright and trembling,
shaking in perfect synchronicity
with me.
We whispered the moon down.
We made a susurration for the stars.
We told each other that when the time came
to let go of our branch
we would hold hands and jump with joy.
But now this, the possibility
that you might jump before me
has me thinking of all the ways
that I can keep you, in gratitude,
in the forest of my heart
and listen any time the wind of your spirit
blows through me
chiming all the leaves within your touch.

Lacy Things

Sometimes the whitest snow falls from the bluest sky as the
sun sinks slowly carrying its shoulder-load of lit firewood
and casting a glow both pink and orange over the cold
fields. Night is coming and the moon will dance in the
empty ballroom of the sky which will be lit by a myriad
celestial candles as she twirls all alone and as the night
deepens she will dance and dance, becoming fainter and
more ethereal – until she resembles the snowflakes that
mirror her from below.

She Wanted Storms

branches shiver
tanka

the trees shiver hard
despite blankets at their feet
their branch-hands can't reach

Annette Marie Smith

The Snow is Made of Pearls

The snow is made of pearls
small and fine and numerous
like the sands of the Great Sea
and if they are a shore
they are a shore that leads to
the back of the North Wind
where every snow scene has its
doppelgänger
globe and is encased and waiting to be
shaken
so that the worlds
(each and every one)
can be stirred
their hearts set all a whirl
with sparkle veils and glitter
sleight of hand.
There is no denying the longing
that feet have for a white path
lined with trees
hung with diamonds
and canopied like a long tunnel
overhung with silks sewn from mists
and embroidered with stars.

Forgiveness Finds Me

Forgiveness finds me
For you
Has been seeking me out
Hard on the scent of my betrayal
Like a hound you set on me
Faithful and undeterred
Forgiveness followed me
Saw through my every ruse and trick
And me
Thinking I am a clever fox
Running
Doubling back and hiding my tracks
Crossing the most barren land
And the greenest flecked bog
To shake you
Here you are anyway with your
Hands on me soothing my ruffled pride
That wouldn't let me see
How fine your fingers
Combing out the brambles would feel to me
And forgiveness, your faithful hound
Has been shut outside the door
Because we don't need him anymore.

Annette Marie Smith

Sanctuary

Framed in sudden shadow from the sinking sun
the leaves, illuminated in groups of 3x4, look like stained
glass windows
that creak and sway upon the trees in the autumn wind.
The day murmurs an evening prayer into the high, neck-
tipping dome
of the cathedral sky while my knees kiss the earth,
and the fingers of the breeze count my hair-strands as
rosaries
and the world around me sighs
in pleasure.
The tree-walls around me seem flagged with goodness
and filled with the song of ancient things
that tilt with me and bow as one
gratefully inclined.

She Wanted Storms

Pluvia

The goddess of rain knows all about your sorrows.
Hasn't she cried your tears with you?
Her voice lulls the tired child in you to sleep,
your fists slowly unclenching, unfurling,
like bow-headed flowers
in a heavy storm.
Her harshness is gentle even as it bruises
and for all the prodding she does
of the soil of your soul
she stirs things up
so that you can bloom again.

Stories the Wind Told Me

She Wanted Storms

Oiseau Chanteur

It was on the first day of June that she started hearing the music. She didn't think much of it at first. It was background noise and very faint as if it came from the neighbor's apartment — as if there was a radio leaning against the wall and crooning.

Now, it is the 23nd day and the music threads itself into the rain that is falling as she makes her way along rue de l'Arbalète in the dark. In the dark she thinks about dark things as the song notes fall around her like golden coins. Her thoughts follow the raindrops in logical progression as they plink their way down to the sewers; make her think of les champignons de Paris (the mushrooms that were formerly grown illegally in the dark tunnels far beneath her feet and fed from the sewage of the tunnels), how they flashed white in the dark like a crop of campaign buttons for hope — how good things can come from crap.

She thinks of how the catacomb city of night (largest necropolis in the world right beneath the city of lights) along with the tunnels beneath her feet are the bony hands of ancestors, in their limestone and gypsum earthworks but also in the actual nests of bones that are to be found down there in a sort of reverse aerie, one that is underground instead of up in the sky. But it is an aerie nonetheless in that it is a place for souls to leap forth from and fly.

But darkest of all, as she walks beneath the rain wavered moon, is the thought that now she knows the meaning of the music she has been hearing and she also knows what she must do.

An ex of hers had said, and it was true, "You never give

93

yourself wholly to me — you always hold something back. I feel that you are never truly mine." It was true. She knew this to be true. There was a part of her soul that sang to the stars at night.

"These kisses are bread crumbs" he said. "And what am I to do with breadcrumbs?" she asked. "Find your way back to me of course" he said. "Well in that case kiss me harder" she said. "For it was not the breadcrumbs, but the pebbles that did the trick in that fairy tale." Afterwards he would whistle a tune that she fell asleep to. It was like a low hum really. It called to her and opened some inner cage even as the cloth of dreams was dropped over her eyes.

Yes, some part of her, in the depths of the night, sang to the stars. And once she was the only one privy to that song. And then it was gone. And then it was back again — as the faintest sound in the background like the sigh of a flower opening, like the overture of champagne bubbles just waiting to be set free from behind their cork. Then stronger and stronger until now — it is all around her in the night. And far above her, la lune looks down in pity.

She arrives at her ex's apartment and yes, just as she expected, the song becomes louder and clearer. She chances a glance through his window as a prelude to knocking on the door and yes again. There he is. He has found it. Given it a nest in his heart.

He has stolen it really with his breadcrumbs and low whistling tune — like a shiny ribbon. Such mundane things have lured that part of her into his arms. "Sneak thief" she says to herself.

How to get it back?

She Wanted Storms

She will start with the parcel of melt-in-your-mouth
macarons that she has carried with her all the way from
Laduree, probably the most famous Parisian patisserie,
where they specialize in the tiny almond flour cakes. Yes.
She will invite him for macarons and coffee and lay some
crumbs of her own.

Finale

And it was established that if he would give her her bird
back she would agree that he could, if it would, have it to
perch on his finger and sing with the understanding that
there was always a place for it ("A gilded cage" she sniffed.
"A bower" he corrected) in his home. In exchange for all of
this — he gave her the moon.

Annette Marie Smith

Anya Sasses Old Man Trouble

"I am plump with the experiences I have had," she says.
"They have not worn me down nor elicited my bones to
peek out from the feathers that I wear."

"And bread and water? I know how to extract the oil from
the surface of the water given me, make one loaf of bread
reach for the heavens in soft sighs and pull an egg out from
behind Disaster's ear whilst nicking Dodgewaith's gold and
pinching Calumny's rear."

She Wanted Storms

The Night You Were Born, Frida Kahlo

Huracan, the storm god, left a quiver of arrows by your cradle. He knew you would want them and he was right, you shot them all your life sometimes even wounding yourself with them.

The parrot-headed one deigned to leave one bright feather by your side. That one feather had all the colors you would ever need but you grew additional feathers of your own reasoning that even a god could not dictate the colors of your art. Besides, he left you only one feather. "Because" he said, "if Frida is given more than one, then will she not be just like us, will she not then also be a god? Let her have this one feather and let her use her feet to get around." So you grew feathers, "Feet," you said "why do I need them, if I have wings to fly?"

A deer came and quietly, while no one was looking, nibbled a portion of your green and tender heart. By the time it was discovered, it was too late. But this too was a gift and intended for your art.

The goddess of beauty gave nothing, only subtracted from the presents piling on the mosaiced floor. She was jealous of the beauty of your spirit and so she took one part of your conventional physical beauty away. She planted wild crows on your brow, a hedge to keep the admirers at bay. But you loved their glossy raucousness, claimed them as a part of you and let them have their say.

The sun wore green for you that day and he has not put that color on for anyone but you. Who can say what it means? You have stated "I never paint dreams or nightmares. I paint my own reality."

97

Annette Marie Smith

The moon traced her finger along your face and whispered two secrets into your tiny shell shaped ears. You always wore earrings to celebrate the things she gave to you.

La Lorna came, uninvited, and left her wet footprints on the tile. Those footprints grew in size, the way hers always do, and ended up as two large pools the color of darkness, the color of sorrowful La Lorna's long black hair. You said "I tried to drown my sorrows but the bastards learned how to swim." Because anything that was your own could not help but strive and thrive and carry on, even things like sorrows.

The Jaguar came and loaned you her soft cough but said you would have to give it back some day.

And there was one more thing that was left for you to have. It has not been determined who left this thing for you, a bag that when opened filled the air with a chalky dust. But this was limestone, a necessary ingredient when building stair-stepped pyramids. And you used this gift to make of yourself a pyramid, a symbol soaring toward the stars. Something that, some say, you sacrificed yourself upon. You said "I leave you my portrait so that you will have my presence all the days and nights that I am away from you."

And so it is.

She Wanted Storms

She Couldn't Trust Doors

She couldn't trust doors even with their hearts of sturdy wood, their shield-like strength, and the way that the grain of their palm caressed her cheek every time she laid it against their surface.

No she couldn't trust them because they had, every one of them, a crack under the door to let all manner of things get in: swirling fogs, dust driven from the rain, sounds off the street, mice on quick pink feet, and worst of all, the sound of footsteps pausing at the door with no knock accompanying.

It was for this reason that she invented the door-bar, not a bar to keep it closed as already could be found, but a bar that fit along the threshold and snugged against the floor.

But what she and her many delighted patrons didn't realize (She ended up making a fortune off her invention. It was just what many had been waiting for.) was that as they kept the impurities out they also hid the light that used to stream in under the cracks. They barred the fresh air that crept in shyly along with the Blattidae and other assorted bugs. The smell of petrichor was denied entrance as was the sound of laughter and the feelings of anticipation that are part of what it means to have a door.

What happened, and there were none to sue and no one left for litigious blame, is that she and her satisfied customers expired in the suffocating confines of what became airless vaults and coffins dark behind closed doors riven of every blemish and which boasted perfect freedom from such and delivered on the claim.

99

Annette Marie Smith

Starched and Monogrammed

He pulled an old-fashioned handkerchief from his perfectly tailored suit breast pocket. It was large and white and was embroidered delicately with his initials: WOE.

Yes, I recognized it as handiwork of my own. WOE and I had been on intimate terms at one time.

I knew conversation, reasoning, would avail for nothing. So I did what I thought best with the handkerchief offered me from his pristine breast. I let it drop to the ground. I noticed as it puffed out its cumulus wings and floated to the ground that it mirrored in a miniature way the canopy of puffery that hung over our heads that day.

Much better, I told myself, when there is nothing left to say – much better to turn on one's heel and leave sir WOE at bay.

She Wanted Storms

The Speckled Ones

This is a story my gran told me about the speckled people. She told it every year on Morgda Eve and as she told it the autumn winds swept the forest floor outside our small home beneath the trees and the trees caught every crisp star in their branches where they lit up the night like a great chandelier.

The speckled people are freckled people: spots of color dotting and dashing their skin. Nowadays this peculiarity is attributed to a substance we all have in our skin in varying degrees and differing manifestations.

But my gran said freckles are the remnants of the markings of a forest people well known in their time but now all but forgotten.

Silent on their feet they were, moving to the whisper of breeze on leaves and windlets on grass. The sighing of the woodland marked their passage through it. Magic it seemed and invisible too because they (like the gray and brown and orange and black array of colors you see in the squirrels and other wild things of fall — matching their colors to the world around them) wore the colors of harvest on themselves and in their skin and thus they blended in so perfectly that they could hardly be detected — whether moving or still. Their "freckles" let them bend in with the fall foliage much like the squirrels and other wildlings.

Their face markings were gold leaf, metallic bronze, tourmaline, and soot. Red bled in lines radiating from their chins and sprawling downward in a path that covered their bodies in green lines and brown, gray and dun. All looked to be painted on but this was their natural coloration.

101

These beings personified the forest in their long twiggy fingers and their bramble hair, their swaying walk and their skin so strange-a-shimmer.

Gran said they were known for their true-seeing into the other world and that the spots on their skin also signified all the possibilities of worlds within worlds.

Well this species of magical being intermarried and over the long years lost much of their distinctiveness but two things remained, my gran always told me, as the wind moaned and the stars twinkled: their spots (now merely freckles) and their unerring ken to true-see." — *Lyssa of the Arboreal Shades from the Night Fairytales series*

She Wanted Storms

Talaya

There are many hard hearts, many hearts of stone in this world. She pulls them up by their mountain roots and carries them, like a load of heart heavy laundry, to the river. She uses the soothing properties of water and in that way she softens the stones.

Her hair is made up of every color in every conceivable (and inconceivable) spectrum and as she launders those hard hearts she cries shining, shimmering, multi-colored pearls of tears.

She polishes the stony hearts to brilliance with her tears and as she does so her hair (each time she does this) is drained of all color. It swirls to her feet like a silver cape and she smiles through her tears.

Her smiles are like kisses that melt in the rain, fleeting but oh so beautiful. As she disappears her hair flames with legion color once again.

Annette Marie Smith

A Pocket Full of Rain

They clung to her like soft overgrown bats, her worries. She kept them close tucked under her arms, sometimes carrying them by their handles, and sometimes she held them over her head a hideous hat if I may say. She was prepared for whatever storms might come her way.

But then one day a real storm came and she threw every black silken concern away. She watched them tumble off into the clouds like spoked tumbleweeds as she began to understand that she could not dance with rain or sing with thunder with all her worries in the way.

Just Another Facebook Post

"A door in an alley. Anyone need a door?" The caption, accompanying a photo of a door, plain, white, and unassuming, propped up against assorted odds and ends in an alley, came across her newsfeed on Facebook and she realized that yes, she did need a door. The friend who posted the photo lived in the next town over. A twenty minute drive to go and fetch a door was doable and, the very next day, done.

Once she had the door in her loft she wasn't sure what she wanted to do with it, where she wanted to put it, etc. But the very fact of having the door imparted a sense of possibility to her. She was an artist and lived her life with a strong, almost religious, sensensitivity to symbolism. She propped it up against the living room wall in between her potted palm tree and her pink velvet couch that was snuggled up against a huge picture window. She knocked on the wood of the door for good luck and turned the handle too, patted it and smiled.

That night, as she lay sleeping, the door creaked open. Someone, or something, came into her loft through the door and stayed until the morning light. It left just as the sun peeked in at the window, closing the door behind it. When she woke up she noticed that the door smelled of fresh paint and was a startling shade of green.

After this she started to sell her work to collectors who were more than casual in their appreciation of her art. In fact they were a bit fanatical and she quickly aquired a small fortune through their dedicated pursuit of the freshness they felt in the presence of her work. (One of her collectors joked about feeling like he could live forever if he could only surround himself with enough of the vitality that was his when he gazed upon her work.)

When the mysterious visitor came next it was in response to her knocking on the door, turning the handle and smiling at herself for her forgotten ritual. The next morning she awoke to the smell of fresh paint and her lucky door (for that was how she thought of it now) was blue.

The happiest time of her life followed in which she fell asleep to blue waves of contentment and woke to what seemed to be the veritable blue bird of happiness perched on the windowsill of her life every day. She did not believe things could get any better for her.

But then she met a writer, an impossibly intriguing man, imposing in his masculine beauty and whose eyes, when she met them as she entered the party, stopped her in her tracks. One thing led to another and she agreed that they should have dinner the next Friday, just the two of them. Getting ready for her date with him she found herself drawn to her door. She gave it three light knocks and a kiss for good luck on its cerulean surface. The outline from her lipstick print beat and blurred like a heart with wings, like Cupid's own signature carved/graffitied against the wooden surface.

After she left the door creaked open and a certain someone, or something, transformed, amid the strong smell of paint, the door to heart's own red.

I will gloss over the way the door changed when her writer went away. He had promised her forever but he really had no say. As unpredictable as one of his own plots, his demise met him as he drove to a book signing. Death had the decency to blush at the aircraft fuselage that had dropped out of the sky and crushed her writer in his small mobile world of car on his way to sign small mobile worlds of books.

I will say only this: the door was gray.
Her door stayed the color of ashes for a very long time. But then one day something wonderful happened. Without a knock, without knuckle provocation in the least, someone, or something, opened the door and when that something left, the door was a yellow that captured all the hope of a rising sun on its grainy visage.

This layer of yellow was followed by one final coat of paint. She awoke to find her door deepening in color, combining all the colors really, into one. As the door darkened to purple, deep brown, and finally black, she reached out her hand, turned the knob, and walked through to the other side.

~~~

"A door in an alley. Anyone need a door?" The caption, accompanying a photo of a door, plain, white, and unassuming, propped up against assorted odds and ends in an alley, came across his newsfeed on Facebook and he realized that yes, he did need a door...

Annette Marie Smith

A Whisker of Doubt

It was always when they were kissing in the dark that it happened. He would feel just the faintest whisper of touch against his face. A tickle really, a butterfly kiss but minus the butterfly. He knew it was not her hands, he held them in his own. He knew it could not be her eyelashes — no matter the length and luxuriousness of them — for they were certainly not located down by her nose. And that was where the slight touch was coming from.

Her eyes he knew and understood, because she had explained it to him so many times, why she had to wear the glasses that fit directly over her eyes propping them open and pinning her long eyelashes above them like feathery black rainbows. The glasses completely covered her eyes like fancy cosplay steampunk goggles and were made of a type of material that was akin to one-way mirror glass. She could see out. Nobody could see in. She took the glasses off in the dark. But underneath the glasses she also wore contact lenses and those she could not take off, even in the dark, she said. He knew that she did though, when he was not around because she had admitted as much to him. "It's not a problem when you're not here." she said.

Whatever it was that was tickling his face did not feel unpleasant. It felt unintentional in its contact and, he had to admit, it even felt nice. He was certainly coming to look forward to the strange interplay of phantom touch against his skin and tried not to think about it too much. He didn't want to get obsessed with it. God forbid he should start to have some sort of fetish for something he was not even sure was there.

In all other respects, this girlfriend of his was perfect.

108

She Wanted Storms

Although he had to admit to himself that she had a crappy work schedule, the midnight shift. So she was out most of the night but when she was there she was everything to him and he felt certain he was becoming everything to her. She positively purred when they lay in each others arms and the dark nibbled quietly around them fraying at the edges between them.

When he said that she purred he meant it. He had never met anyone who snored like her — in the exact manner of a cat purring, like rocks tumbling over and over down the long velvet slope of her throat. Tumbling down and back up, up and back down, repeatedly. And then there was the fact that she did have odd taste in clothing. It wasn't just the goggles. She wore a skintight suit of fur, so soft and glossy, so petal yielding to his touch. He liked the way it felt as she stretched up against him. But he had to admit that the fur suit was a little weird. And it was also a little weird that she never took it off.

And now, now he was brought to a point that made his heart beat fast at the duplicity involved. He couldn't help himself in showing off his girl to his buddies when they were out for beers at O'Geary's (best Irish pub in town).

She had sent him a selfie, her black nails dark against the pale of her face as she held the goggles with one pinky out in a salute of sorts. In the subject she had put "For Psykey, only for Psykey, me." But her face was obscured in the photo by the shadow of the goggles and her hand against them and he couldn't display her face to his content. And therein too was the problem. His buddies wanted to see a photo of her face clear and unimpeded by shadows and goggles and sharp black nails. This opened up the whole can of worms about how she never took her goggles off

109

unless it was dark, it brought up her fur suit, it brought up everything.

No matter how happy he professed to be with her, his two friends (they were really more like brothers since they had grown up in each other's houses) were doubtful of the wisdom of being with someone who wouldn't take off her goggles in the light.

"Wow. How do you even know her? Eyes are important man." Buddy #1 said.

"Dude. You owe it to yourself to be able to look into the eyes of the chick you're banging." Buddy #2 said.

And so these two friends of his, before they left the bar to go back to the bachelor apartment they shared, convinced him that there was something not quite right with the way things were going with him and Erosa. With their questions and their skeptical looks they had firmly introduced — a whisker of doubt.

The next time he was out for beers with his buddies, things had not changed for Psykey and Erosa. Six months into living together and he was still luxuriating in the lap of feeling happiness and contentment. She was still perfect in almost every way. And best yet so far, she had promised him that if he could wait for six more months, she would — yes — she would take the goggles off for him. "Just be patient Psykey and everything will work out for you and me." she said. He could hardly fall asleep that night he was so excited about Erosa's concession. Soon though, as always happened, the low purr of her snore lulled him to sleep. Happy and content.

She Wanted Storms

So when he told his buddies that he would finally see her without her goggles in six months time he was rudely surprised at their reactions.

"No way would I wait." Buddy #1 said. "This is getting seriously weird."

"You've been together six months and she's still pulling that weird crap?" Buddy #2 said. "Dump her, bro. Dump her."

Psykey had a new photo of Erosa but he didn't have the heart to show it to his buddies. It showed her from behind, her fur bodysuit hugging her curves, her waist-length black hair tumbling down her back as she bent over the long length of her own legs and looked back over her shoulder at him through her goggles. Those damned goggles.

And so it was that he found himself at his buddies' urging, not dumping her, but putting into action a plan that had every reason to be successful. It was sure to succeed and sure to finally allay his suspicions. So Psykey didn't know why his heart felt so heavy as he made his way home. The plan was simple. When Erosa fell into her deep sleep exactly at 2:00 am, the sleep it was impossible to wake her from (he knew because he had tried so many times), he would take off her goggles himself and put all this nonsense that there was something wrong with Erosa to bed.

It was midnight when he got in and Erosa came in shortly after. He looked at her with her secrets and her mysteries and her unbelievable beauty and (almost) perfect self and for a minute he really hated her. Hated her so much that he felt the urge to leave and never have to look at her beauty and her goggles again. But she slipped up to him and slid her arms around him and tiptoed up to place a kiss against

111

his cheek, his chin, his eyes (which were now closed), his ears, his neck. When she finally got to his mouth they were in bed and he could no more have left than pulled pastrami out of his left ear at that point. And then he felt the whisper of touch against his face and he fell in love with her all over again. And he thought to himself as he drifted off to sleep that she really was perfect — not just almost perfect, but perfect.

Her soft purring woke him and he looked blurrily at the bedside clock to see that right on schedule Erosa had fallen asleep at 2:00 am. Without really meaning to he got up and turned on the overhead light. Without thinking about it he walked over to Erosa and slowly, almost tenderly, rolled her over onto her stomach and undid the clasp of the goggles. He rolled her back onto her back and saw that even with the clasp having been undone the goggles remained affixed, almost as if they were suction stuck. He reached down and with steady hands grasped the protuberances of the goggles, one in each hand, and pulled.

Looking down at her with the offending goggles in his hands he had to ask himself "Now what?" The innocent skin of two perfectly normal eyelids lay beneath his gaze. She looked so vulnerable, so naked in a way that he had never experienced with her before. This was such an intimate moment and it suddenly occurred to him how wrong that the intimacy was happening without her consent.

He took her into his arms as he laid down beside her with the intention of putting the goggles back on her in just one more minute's time. He stroked the ravens of her hair, nest and birds and song all twined into one glorious mess that hair, and gazed with a feeling of dread at the perfect blamelessness of her sleeping eyes until he fell asleep.

She Wanted Storms

A long drawn out hiss woke Psykey. He opened his eyes to see a monster beside him in bed. Erosa was staring at him with the slit pupiled eyes of cat. Staring and snarling, snarling and staring. Fu manchu whiskers quivered from her cheeks and arrowhead fangs parted her lips. Her black nails had elongated into what can only be described as claws and completed the Cat Woman on steroids look that he saw before him. The hiss ended in a growl and she leapt. Psykey ducked but Erosa had leapt not at him — but from the bed.

She let out a long wail and then all cat semblance melted away and Erosa morphed into perfection right before his eyes.

"Take your last look at me, Psykey. If only you had been patient. If only you had waited. Six more months and the curse that I have been carrying of being a shape shifter would have been lifted. It has been disappearing with only the shadows of it clinging to me at night. I haven't been wearing the contact lenses that protected my eyes for weeks. Our love was destroying the curse. I could have been with you all of the time as you see me now. Why, Psykey? Why?"

Before he could answer, she disappeared in a special effects storm of light sparks and left him with the phantom feel of whiskers that he knew were no longer there.

113

Annette Marie Smith

Constant Melusine

The woman is always naked and there is always a snake,
whether it is tester, taster, tamer, whether it is part of her
person in gleaming scale tail and the snake is colored green.
There is always the undulation of mystery unveiling and a
twisting this way and that of thoughts revolving upon
themselves, figure eights of intuitions making patterns in
the what-if dust, the could-be dirt, that is at the woman's
feet and that has always been.

She uses everything she has, the excrescence of her self that
she emits with sweat. She gives everything she has and this
giving is always in the nature of birthing, relying wholly on
herself she labors making something beautiful out of that
which was not.

She loves the things she makes in an idolatrous way,
transfuses them with her spirit, hallows them with her
heart. She creates them in her image but it is a mirror
image, her face's remembered reflection in rippled stream,
her proportions limned by wavering waterfalls with
rainbows overarching inspiring her paints.

And there are always more tears, of joy, of sorrow,to make
more waterfalls and rivers and streams, watery deeps and
wellsprings of desire. She is as much fountain as anything
else and that is why she has been called Naiad, Scylla,
Melancholy, Melusine.

And Melusine, gowned in golden scales, shimmers before
the collective eye in every little Eve. Hisses of adoration, or
accusation, writhe in the wake of her feet–when she wears
them.

114

She Wanted Storms

She is always with us, constant Melusine, cavorting in a pool the color of milk beneath red-roofed forest trees. The trees themselves are red and gold but Melusine is green, green, always ever-green.

Promises

The wolves kept their word that night and for every night thereafter, through countless nights and long years until their mortal eyes could watch over her no more. But by that time they, and she, had become something larger than their original selves.

She became the very pith of vulnerability, a goddess in her own right, Fides Quae, whose strength lay in the fragile line, like an exposed throat, of trust. The wolves leapt into the heavens and became the constellation Lupus Immortalis.

Their eyes glitter with all the endurance of diamonds lit with the fire of wild hearts in the eternal night of space. They watch over the hearts of those that despite having every reason to be wary, give themselves to trust in the same way that a sleeper gives herself to dreams.